This edition published by Parragon Books Ltd in 2014

Parragon Books Ltd
Chartist House
15–17 Trim Street
Bath BA1 1HA, UK
www.parragon.com

Copyright © 2014 Disney Enterprises, Inc.
www.disneyfairies.co.uk

ISBN 978-1-4723-8575-8

Printed in China

DISNEY FAIRIES

TinkerBell
AND THE
LEGEND OF THE
NEVERBEAST

PaRragon

Bath · New York · Cologne · Melbourne · Delhi
Hong Kong · Shenzhen · Singapore · Amsterdam

On a night like no other, as
Iridessa gathered light beams,
a mysterious green comet
streaked across the sky.

Ancient fairy lore told that
the very same comet had
appeared nearly a thousand
years before.

The green light from the comet
spilled into the dark corners of a
deep cave ... where bright eyes opened
and something stirred!

The next morning, Tinker Bell delivered a wagon that she had made from a basket to her friend Fawn.

Fawn was secretly looking after a baby hawk in her house. As hawks were considered dangerous animals by the fairies, she wanted to use the basket wagon to sneak it out of Pixie Hollow so she didn't alarm anyone.

With the hawk hidden under berries in the basket, Fawn and Tink cautiously pulled the wagon through Pixie Hollow. But Rosetta offered to help move the berries by sprinkling pixie dust on them. They floated up to reveal Fawn's friend.

"HAWK!" screamed a terrified fairy.

The scout fairies, who are the protectors of Pixie Hollow, appeared and Nyx, their leader, captured the bird under a net.

"Let her go," demanded Fawn.

Nyx scowled. "We'll handle this."

Queen Clarion arrived to see what was going on. "Is everyone alright?"

It wasn't the first time that Fawn had brought a dangerous animal to Pixie Hollow.

The queen smiled at Fawn. "You've always let your heart be your guide, but...."

"But I also need to listen with my head," said Fawn. "Next time, I promise, I will."

The following day, Fawn decided to be a model animal fairy by teaching bunnies to hop. In the middle of the class she heard a loud groan come from deep in the forest.

Even though she knew she should stay out of trouble, she decided to investigate and found herself at the entrance of a cave.

"Come on," she told herself. "Listen to your head. Your heart gets you into trouble."

But Fawn was too curious and flew into the darkness of the cave.

Fawn cautiously made her way to the bottom of the
deep cave. There lay a huge animal unlike anything she
had ever seen before.

"What are you?" she wondered to herself.

Suddenly, the beast looked straight at her and stood up.
Without warning, the creature let out a furious,
ground-shaking roar!

Fawn fled the cave as fast as her wings could carry her.

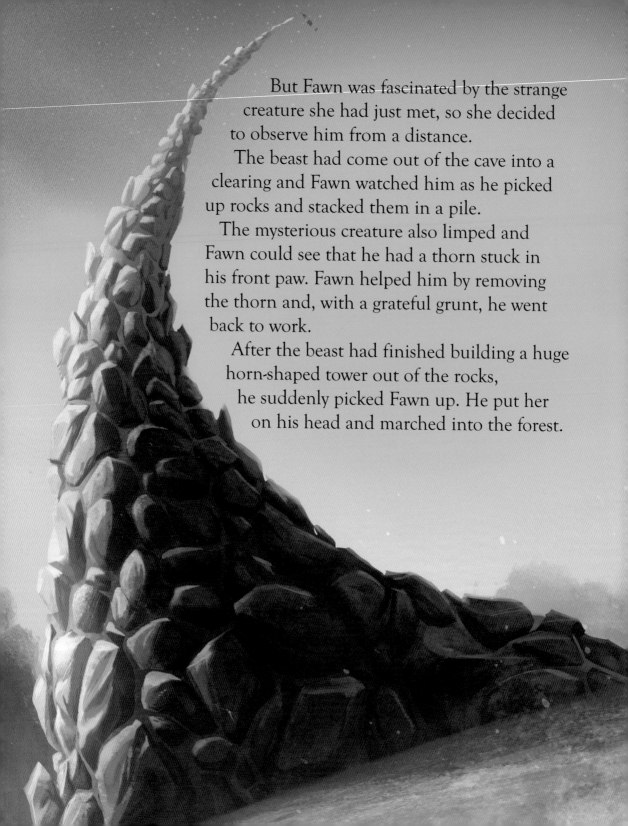

But Fawn was fascinated by the strange
creature she had just met, so she decided
to observe him from a distance.
    The beast had come out of the cave into a
clearing and Fawn watched him as he picked
up rocks and stacked them in a pile.
    The mysterious creature also limped and
Fawn could see that he had a thorn stuck in
his front paw. Fawn helped him by removing
the thorn and, with a grateful grunt, he went
 back to work.
    After the beast had finished building a huge
horn-shaped tower out of the rocks,
    he suddenly picked Fawn up. He put her
    on his head and marched into the forest.

Fawn stayed with the beast, who she named 'Gruff', and watched him build several tall towers with large rocks. She wanted to find out more about him and the towers he was building.

After she'd spent some time with Gruff, she realized that he wasn't dangerous and decided to introduce him to her friends. "Ladies, say hello to Gruff."

Tinker Bell and the other fairies gasped when they saw the creature hanging from a tree. Fawn told the fairies about her plan.

"I'm going to take him to the queen so she can see that he's harmless."

But when Fawn arrived at Queen Clarion's house, the queen was talking with Nyx. The head scout fairy had found ancient drawings of the comet. According to the legend of the NeverBeast, the last time the comet appeared, it awakened a monster that had destroyed Pixie Hollow with lightning.

Nyx explained to Fawn and the queen that she planned to capture the monster in order to protect Pixie Hollow.

Back in the forest, Fawn explained to her friends what Nyx had told them. "Nyx thinks Gruff is a monster. Crazy, right?"

The next morning, the fairies in Pixie Hollow awoke to a strange sight. Thick, green clouds blanketed the sky. As Tink looked up she saw the scout fairies fly off, armed and carrying a net.

Tink gasped. She knew they were going after Gruff.

When Fawn went to look for Gruff, he was gone. Tink arrived and told Fawn about the scout fairies and they both realized they needed to find Gruff, quick!

Tink suggested they split up. According to the legend, the NeverBeast needed to build more rock towers in the Autumn and Winter Woods.

Tink decided to head straight to the Winter Woods and found the NeverBeast there. Just as she was about to warn him, Gruff swatted her to the ground.

Fawn arrived and found Tink, who was knocked out. "Gruff, what did you do?"

Suddenly, lightning struck a rock tower and Fawn watched Gruff transform. Horns grew out of his head and a hump formed on his back. He looked like a monster!

Fawn coaxed Gruff out into the open and the scout fairies threw a net over him! She was worried that Gruff was dangerous so she had reluctantly helped Nyx to capture her friend.

"Nightshade powder!" called Nyx. The powder was thrown over Gruff and he became drowsy and fell to the ground.

Fawn went to check on Tink, who had woken up after she was taken to Fairy Urgent Care.

"I'm so sorry," said Fawn.

"There is nothing to be sorry for," Tink replied. She explained that the lightning had hit a tree and it nearly fell on her, but Gruff pushed her out of the way just in time. He'd saved her life!

"And I betrayed him," said Fawn, as she left in a hurry.

Fawn was joined by her friends and they flew through the growing storm to set Gruff free by releasing him from the scout fairies' net. He couldn't see properly because of the nightshade powder, so they led him to one of the rock towers he had built.

Suddenly, lightning bounced off the tower and hit Gruff's horns. The fairies watched as huge wings grew out of his back.

Fawn now understood Gruff's purpose. "He's not here to shoot lightning at Pixie Hollow," she announced. "He's here to draw it away!"

Fawn led Gruff to the towers. At each one, lightning leaped from the tower to Gruff's horns and he absorbed the electrical energy.

Soon there was only one tower to go!

Fawn and Gruff reached the final
tower when Nyx knocked it down!
Gruff fell to the ground and the
lightning that was being focused
on his horns split into lots of
smaller bolts and lit trees across
Pixie Hollow on fire.

"Nyx!" cried Fawn. "What are you doing?"

"Saving Pixie Hollow," Nyx yelled.

Just then, Nyx was almost hit by lightning, but Gruff stepped in front of her and absorbed the strike.

Nyx finally understood that Gruff was trying to save Pixie Hollow, but it was too late to repair the final tower. As they looked at the sky, Fawn realized that all the lightning was coming from one spot. She turned to Gruff. "Follow me."

Fawn sped to the centre of the storm and Gruff followed closely behind. As they got closer, Gruff pushed Fawn out of harm's way and the lightning was drawn to his horns.

Gruff gathered up the storm's energy. Then, suddenly ... BOOM! There was an enormous blast. The storm was over.

Gruff was a hero. In the days that followed, he helped the fairies repair the damage caused by the storm.

The fairies wanted Gruff to stay, but Fawn knew it wasn't possible after she listened to his chest and heard his heart getting slower. "His work is done. He needs to go back into hibernation."

Fawn and her fairy friends led Gruff back to his cave. Hundreds of fairies from Pixie Hollow turned up to say goodbye and wish him well.

Tinker Bell had made him a special bed and Rosetta gave him a fluffy pillow.

Fawn tucked the NeverBeast in and kissed him on the nose. It was time to say goodbye to the best friend she'd ever had. "I'm really going to miss you. I love you, Gruff."

And with that, Gruff's big eyes closed and he drifted off to sleep. But the fairies knew that, one day, he'd be back.